The Very Worst Thing

by Berthe Amoss

Parents' Magazine Press · New York

For Jimmy

REPORT -TOM
REDDING - A
ARITHMETIC. A
GEOGRAPHY. A
CONDUCT A

FOR TOM

There are good things

and bad things,

terrible things,

and worse things,

but the very worst thing of all was when
I was the new boy on the first day of school.

I sneaked into a desk at the back,
but Miss Prue saw me.
"Welcome, Thomas," she said. "Let's all welcome
Thomas, everyone! Thomas is our new boy!"

My name is Tom. No one calls me Thomas
except my grandfather.
"Hello, Thomas," said the girls.
"Welcome, Toe-mas," said Mr. Smarty.

Everyone except me had the book from last year.
I had to share — with Alice.

Also, the paint spilled on the sweater my mother
knitted one size larger to grow on.

Henry lent me the handkerchief *his* mother
makes him take for emergencies.
Henry has a snake in a cage at home.

There was an election of class officers
and I was elected—

Sanitation Chief.

At recess they chose teams.

We used to play *baseball* at my old school.

No one here saw me hit that homer last year.

And I made a mistake looking for the boys' room.

Jim said, Shucks, when he was new, he accidentally
walked into the teachers' lounge. And there was
Miss Prue with her shoes off!

Henry said, Well, once he bumped into the principal
and the principal said, *"Watch where you're going!"*

Horace said, *That* was nothing. Once he opened
a little glass door and pulled a handle, and

the whole fire department came clanging up
in the middle of arithmetic class!

I found out that everyone brings his lunch to school in a paper bag and buys milk or soda.

No one brings a hard-boiled egg.

I also found William, the other new boy.

Hi, TOM, TOM, Hi!

HEY, TOM!

TOM!

And my little brother.

Luckily, Horace had an extra peanut-butter and jelly.

Horace raises mice. So do I.

One thing just like my old school is—

I am the shortest boy in class.

William said, He was the shortest boy once,
but that after his tonsils were removed,

he grew two inches in two months.

april 1   april 15   may 1   may 15

June 1

He has his tonsils in a jar and he is going to bring
them to school for Show and Tell.

Horace and I asked Miss Prue if she wanted us to bring
our mice, and she said that would be interesting.
Henry wanted to bring his snake,
but Miss Prue said that would be *too* interesting
because snakes eat mice and Henry would have to wait
his turn—after Alice shows her foreign dolls and Elizabeth
tells how she makes fudge with Rice Krispies.

The best thing about yesterday at school was the bell.

Walking home, I found out that Mr. Smarty lives on my block.

We threw a ball around.

His real name is John.

I ate a banana mayonnaise peanut-butter
sandwich, put on my good old gray sweatshirt,
and went over to John's to see his tree house.
Horace rode up, and we started a club called
the JH&T Club—for John, Horace and Tom.

Jim and Henry got in today, so the J and H stand
for them, too. But now William wants to belong.
He says the T can stand for tonsils and he will give
his to the club.

So tomorrow, after the bell, we're going to William's house for the first meeting.

And the very best thing is — the very worst thing is over!

BERTHE AMOSS was born in New Orleans, Louisiana, and is a graduate of Newcomb College (Tulane University) where she studied art and English literature. Her first picture book, *It's Not Your Birthday*, which she wrote and illustrated, was published in 1966.

To date, she has four picture books on the Parents' Magazine Press list: *By the Sea* (a book without words), *The Marvelous Catch of Old Hannibal, Old Hasdrubal and the Pirates*, and *The Very Worst Thing*. Mrs. Amoss is married to Walter James Amoss, Jr. and they have six sons. Their home is in New Orleans.